THE Christmas Color

WORDS AND PICTURES BY TORI HIGA

The Christmas Color
Text and Illustrations copyright © 2020 Tori Higa
ISBN-Hardcover: 978-1-7332828-6-4
ISBN-Softcover: 978-1-7332828-7-1
Library of Congress Control Number: 2020943476

Published by Little Lamb Books
www.littlelambbooks.com
P.O. Box 211724, Bedford, TX 76095

All rights reserved. No part of this book may be reproduced, distributed, or transmitted in any form or manner whatsoever without the prior written permission from the publisher, except in the case of brief quotation embodied in critical articles and reviews and certain other noncommercial uses permitted by copyright law.

Ordering information: Special discounts available on quantity purchases by associations, non-profits, and others. For details, contact the publisher at the address above.

Scriptures taken from the Holy Bible, New International Version, NIV.
Copyright ©1973, 1978, 1984, 2011 by Biblica, Inc.
Used by permission of Zondervan. All rights reserved worldwide. www.zondervan.com
The NIV and New International Version are trademarks registered
in the United States Patent and Trademark Office by Biblica, Inc.

Written and Illustrated by Tori Higa, www.torihiga.com
Edited by Lindsay Schlegel, www.lindsayschlegel.com
Cover Design by Lisa Vega, www.lisaevega.com

Visit www.littlelambbooks.com for a variety of educational resources for teachers and librarians.

First Edition
Printed and bound in USA

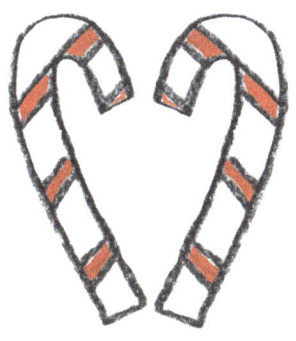

For my Dad:
Westy, I will always cherish being your daughter.
Thank you for a lifetime of unconditional love,
And thank you for believing this book could be a
book right from the start.

THIS BOOK BELONGS TO:

_____

I've no doubt you've often heard it said
That the color of Christmas is

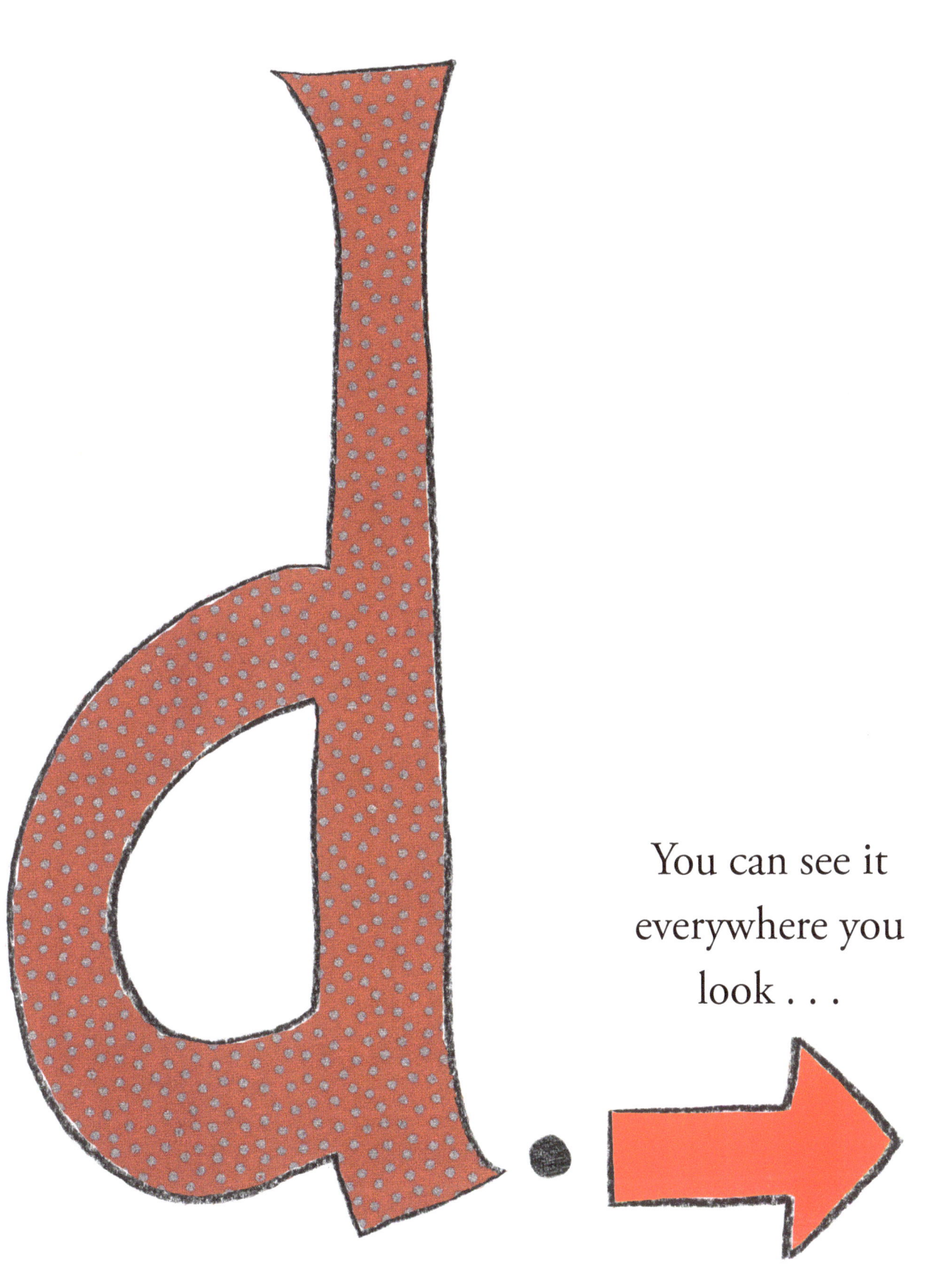

You can see it everywhere you look . . .

In the biggest house

and smallest nook.

Is it because of Santa's red clothes?

Or maybe it's Rudolph's shiny red nose?

Could it be the red berries we pick?

Cocoa with a red peppermint stick?

Pretty red paper used to gift wrap?

Your favorite red mittens and wool cap?

The red stockings we hang by the fire?
Or the poinsettias we so admire?

The bright red bulbs that light up our trees?
No, something else brings us to our knees.

Jesus was born that first Christmas day.
In a manger, surrounded by hay.
When He died and rose, His blood was shed.
And that is why we have Christmas red.

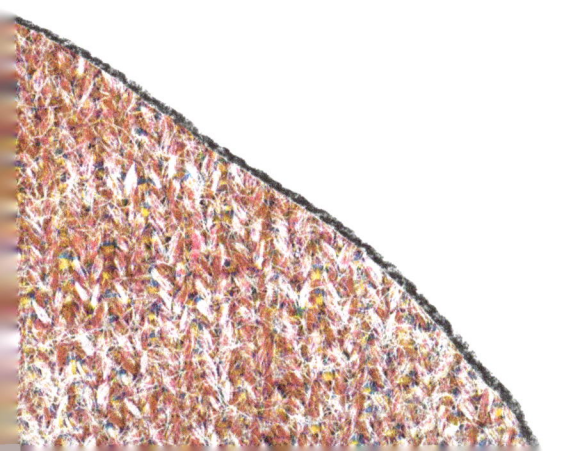

We love the lights, trim, and all the fun,
But those things only point to the One.

His salvation is yours to receive.
All you must do is simply believe.

In this busy and festive season,
Don't forget Jesus is the reason.

And tonight, when you lay down your head,
Rejoice: the Christmas color is red.

TORI HIGA is inspired by her faith, family and friends, coffee shops, people watching, and all things vintage. She loves making art, and has created pieces for everything from carpet patterns to greeting cards to wall art. Recently, with kids in mind, Tori began pairing her pictures with the words she writes. She currently lives in Southern California with her husband, Branden, two kids, Kai and Maile, and a puppy named Edie. Tori considers it an honor to make books and inspire kids in the ways of the Lord. *The Christmas Color* is her debut children's book. You can visit her website at www.torihiga.com.

CPSIA information can be obtained
at www.ICGtesting.com
Printed in the USA
LVHW022320070121
675506LV00011B/227